Almost
Japanese

Also available in

SCRIBNER **SIGNATURE** EDITIONS

ON EXTENDED WINGS *by Diane Ackerman*

GROWING UP RICH *by Anne Bernays*

SOUTH STREET *by David Bradley*

THE TENNIS HANDSOME *by Barry Hannah*

WHAT I KNOW SO FAR *by Gordon Lish*

DEAR MR. CAPOTE *by Gordon Lish*

ELBOW ROOM *by James Alan McPherson*

THE MISFITS AND OTHER STORIES *by Arthur Miller*

VOICES AGAINST TYRANNY *edited by John Miller*

COOL HAND LUKE *by Donn Pearce*

BLOOD TIE *by Mary Lee Settle*

THE LOVE EATERS *by Mary Lee Settle*

THE KISS OF KIN *by Mary Lee Settle*

THE CLAM SHELL *by Mary Lee Settle*

20 UNDER 30 *edited by Debra Spark*

STATE OF GRACE *by Joy Williams*

Almost Japanese

A NOVEL BY

SARAH SHEARD

Sarah Sheard

SCRIBNER SIGNATURE EDITION

CHARLES SCRIBNER'S SONS · NEW YORK
1987

Library of Congress Cataloging-in-Publication Data

Sheard, Sarah.
Almost Japanese.

(Scribner signature edition)
I. Title.
PR9199.3.S5115A79   1987   813'.54   86-24797
ISBN 0-684-18805-8
ISBN 0-684-18806-6 (pbk.)

Originally published in paperback by The Coach House Press,
Toronto, Canada

First Scribner Signature Edition in 1987
Copyright © 1985 Sarah Sheard
All rights reserved

Printed and bound by Fairfield Graphics,
Fairfield Pennsylvania

Cover art: Morning, *by Francesco Clemente.*
Courtesy of Thomas Amman.

For my folks.

Special thanks to Margaret Atwood and
Michael Ondaatje for their meticulous reading
and *Banzai!* encouragement, Stan Bevington
for blind faith, Val Frith for jasmine high teas,
Maya Koizumi for lore, Masumi Suzuki for
calligraphy, Roy Kiyooka for insisting I write
from the heart and to D.Y. who shared the
secrets of Discipline and Passion.

'What one respects must be perfect.'

Who was I before all this happened? I am trying to remember.

Feet

They left two parallel tracks in the snow as each parent took an arm and dragged me like a sack to nursery school. One morning, after two weeks of this, I suddenly announced that I would walk.

My father came home that night with a gauzy sack of chocolate coins in his briefcase.

Nose

The woody smell of the arrowroot biscuits on a flowered plate at nursery school. The oilskin tablecloth covered with glasses of apple juice. The starchy smell of fingerpaints drying on my smock, a cut-down shirt of my father's.

More nose

I am in Sunday school. Our church is on the membrane between a rich neighbourhood and a working-class one and I am feeling self-conscious in my scratchy Sunday best. A little girl with dirty legs smiles at me as she steps across me on the floor and I catch a sour smell. I point her out to my mother later and she tells me that God doesn't like to hear those things in His house.

Hips

My first costume was a kilt my mother bought me to wear to kindergarten. I preferred costumes to ordinary clothes and began to make my own out of tea-towels, dustrags, my father's old pyjama top.

Skin

When my father came home he always put his briefcase on the chair in the front hall. I was not allowed to open it but I liked to wrap my hand around the stitched leather handle which grew darker over the years. When the stitching unravelled, a bone of metal poked through. A witch's finger.

Ears

I am squatting to watch the drops gather along the seam in the ceiling. A drop of water fattens and falls with a pat onto the damp halo of newspaper around my mother's shoes.

Arms and legs

I got up on a chair. Reached for the five-pound bag of flour, broke it open and shook it out. Lay down and made angels, lots of them, all over the kitchen floor. For mom, when she got back.

Vocal chords

My mother, on her way out shopping, gave me her old muskrat coat to play with. I got out her black-handled scissors, cut open the coat and sewed pieces, inside out, into Indian leggings, complete with fringe. I was upstairs, admiring the effect in the mirror, when I heard her come in the front door, discover the remains scattered across the kitchen table, shriek my name. Just once.

Face (loss of)

The class photograph is passed from desk to desk. Little sighs of suppressed laughter. Something is happening. When the picture is handed to me it is terrible to see. Little pin-holes all over my face, felt through the back like voodoo braille. Why only my face? The whole class hates me.

My hands tremble holding it out to my mother. She looks hard at it for a moment and begins to laugh – the kids did this to you? She pulls me to her, her vibrations shaking open my clenched-fist heart. It IS funny. She gasps out – Oh, the things kids do to one another. Would you ever be that cruel?

I stop in mid-laugh, look up at her, open-mouthed.

Hands

My mother kisses my fingers goodbye through the letterbox.

Skull and bones

I pulled the covers up to my chin and rolled onto my back. From my bed by the window sill, I could see the stars straight above me. It was like sleeping outside but much cosier. A soft rain began to fall and the window sill gave off a damp wood-work smell. My sheets and pillow smelled good and I listened to the water gurgling down the eavestrough. It was at that moment, feeling so safe and peaceful, when suddenly another feeling swept over me – of disappearing into the darkness, of my parents, of everyone alive vanishing, rolling out the window, evaporating like rain. Death was night that lasted forever. How much time did I have before I turned into mud and got rained on and walked over by strangers?

Before skull and bones?

She turned from the sink to answer me, holding up a potato-peeling. You were this. You were a tomato in a sack. You were the dust blowing around the corner before you were born.

Nipples

Bruna, who cleaned our house, loved to startle me out of a sound sleep at the crack of dawn on Saturday mornings, whipping the covers off me and stripping the bed while the sheets were still warm.

Bruna!

I lunged for them back but a second too late.

She saw everything! I was sleeping naked, like a movie star!

Neighbours

A senator and his wife lived on my street. The widow of a famous man lived two doors down. She was addressed as Lady B. A chauffeur did her shopping. Up the hill on the corner, Mr G. lived with his sister and their old nursemaid. In a house that looked like a French hotel with turrets and a balcony that wrapped all the way around. Gardeners came twice a month to feed the roses. Mr G. kept an Alsatian, Rudi, to guard him. When Rudi died, another dog took its place. A succession of Rudis, fierce and unpredictable, threw themselves against the fence every time I walked to and from school.

Eyes

When I was in grade three my father decided to build a fountain in the back yard, drawing kids in from blocks away. Other kids' fathers didn't do things like fountains. He showed us where he planned to dig, marking it with a ring of bricks. He pointed out where he would bury the pump. When he began to shovel, we could see how ropey his muscles showed under his work-shirt.

He unearthed insects and wrigglers we'd never seen before. Flatworms and millipedes with legs that glittered as they frantically reburied themselves. My father told us the sun burnt them. He showed us ants' eggs, grains of rice piled up neatly with black seeds showing through the glaze. He picked some up between his fingers to show we shouldn't be afraid and although it revolted us he put an egg into every outstretched palm and we squealed as he did it but he was right. They were earth hearts, halfway between dirt and being alive.

He finished the hole the next day. He lined it with heavy plastic, then began to lay bricks over top that, straightening up now and again to survey the effect. It looked like four walls in the ground. A nest of brick eggs. Nothing like the ornamental fountain in Peppio's Italian restaurant where I'd been taken for my birthday. Then he installed the pipe and hose that connected to the pump and the fountain began to take shape. He dug another hole and buried the pump. I lifted one end of the scalp of sod he'd removed and he took the other and we swung it back into place over the wound in the lawn and my mother claimed she couldn't spot it from her kitchen window, we'd done such a good job. After the mortar had dried and been waterproofed with a compound that stank and made us dizzy he ran the garden hose and filled the pool and all the kids who'd been watching took their socks and shoes off and paddled. It was so cold it made our bones ache but it was our very own swimming-pool. My father sent my mom off to buy goldfish.

It was time to plug in the pump. A big kid picked up the extension cord to the buried pump, ran up the hill to the garage, through the window, and plugged it into the outlet behind the car.

The lawn gargled.

A rude string of farts broke out of the top of the pipe, then a rusty ball of water wobbled and rose into a dramatic plume. My father undid the baggie of goldfish, ornamental fantails, and we all leaned over to watch him pour them in. They looked fantastic, their fins undulating like pony-tails underwater – except they were swimming a little jerkily, all in the same direction, tumbling head over heels in the undertow towards the yawning intake pipe and then suddenly we only counted five instead of six and then three and then –

My father dashed up the lawn to cut the motor but it was too late. A kid yelled and pointed. There on the wobbling ball of water danced little glinty bits of fish. Pink and gold. A fin, a head, part of a tail. The pieces floated into a quiet corner of the pool and we all watched silently as my father fetched the kitchen sieve and scooped the bits out onto a sheet of newspaper.

After dinner, I looked out my bedroom window onto the fountain and saw there was hardly any water left. The fountain was giving off a dry, rasping sound as it sucked on air. But the Bennetts' garden, below ours, looked like a rice paddy.

My father worked on that pool all summer long. He tore out the bricks and laid in more plastic, re-bricked it and caulked the whole thing over with flexible rubber. Then concrete, fibreglass and turquoise pool-paint. It still leaked like crazy. The fountain drew in on itself. When it ran now, it gave off a dull, flat sound and the hose was kept running continuously to top it up. Compensating for evaporation, Dad said. That fall, when the ground froze, the whole rim of bricks heaved itself up on end, a jawful of laughing teeth.

The following spring, my father filled the pool in with dirt, leaving the rim of bricks as they were. The grass seeded itself over the dirt and clay and my mother planted bleeding-heart bushes in the middle. The fountain is still visible, years later, imbedded in the lawn like the miniature remains of a Scottish castle.

That water wanted out. And it got out. Water was a natural teacher.

My name is Emma. A simple one. Two syllables. Non-ethnic.

One night, my parents had a dinner party, and before the guests arrived my father decided to paint the front door. While my mother and I glided about the kitchen, polishing glasses, sorting out the cutlery, turned bread out of pans, brushed butter onto food, my father began methodically spreading newspapers over the front porch. He unscrewed the Medusa's-head door-knocker, dropped her in Brasso, and began to paint. The dog discovered the opened can of black enamel and nosed the lid off the edge of the porch into the garbage pail, by which time the light was starting to fail, so my father rigged a bulb on a long extension cord from the living-room, down the front hall, through the porch and out the door. Just a little too late to catch the panpipe rill of black enamel hardening along the bottom of the door.

I lit the candles. My mother retreated upstairs to dress. The dog, intoxicated by the fumes, began dancing and growling at the umbrella-stand. Dad printed a caution sign and strung it up across the porch, but it was unreadable in the gloom and the first guest ducked the string, pushed open the door and discovered the paint on his palm just after he'd embraced my mother.

After the clean-up, I stowed solvent and rag in a can at the top of the cellar stairs where an inebriated guest, searching for the bathroom, inadvertently opened the door and drop-kicked the can downstairs into the loaded laundry basket.

★

The empty Chrysler, family car, coasts past us down the driveway like a dream. My father lopes after it, his arms like a sleepwalker's, reaching for the wheel through the open window, but the car glides out of reach and he stops in the forsythia shadow to watch the double doors of the garage crumple inward like wet biscuit.

When I open my eyes again, my mother and father are disappearing through the perfectly-shaped hole in the wood.

This was the third, and last, time the car ran away.

★

My father wasn't sure about a private school. He didn't want his daughter turning into a conformist. But it was the uniform that made me want to go. Kilt, blazer, tie-pin, knee-socks, black oxfords. Like a business suit. That, and the fact that it was so close by. I could come home every day for lunch.

And no boys.

Thirteen. No blood yet.

19

The approach *(kyohan)* to a bridge.

We were getting a new symphony conductor! And he was Japanese. Very exotic. An exciting young discovery, the papers were calling him. His arrival coincided with my fourteenth birthday so, as a present, my parents took me to his opening concert.

When a slight figure, in knife-thin tails and a mass of hair, darted onstage to the podium, we stood up to applaud him. He bowed and we took our seats.

The overture began. His movements, his hair, his face. I couldn't take my eyes off him. All the way home, I sat in the back seat, rereading his biography on the symphony programme, looking at his photo, listening to my parents' exclamations about his long hair, his graceful conducting, his reputation.

I kept savouring his name, Akira Tsutsuma, exotic syllables in my mouth.

When he bought the Bennetts' house next door, my parents said he was a genius. It would be like living next door to Marconi or Einstein! They said geniuses were born only a few times every century. Special people, touched by God. Geniuses probably experienced everything differently from normal people. Every day I'd be walking on a sidewalk that he walked on.

Don't envy him, my father said. He's separated from other people because of his gift. It's a huge responsibility. He's probably alone a lot. He has to work a lot harder than ordinary people, suffer tons of pressure.

I remembered reading about Schubert, who bubbled over with inspiration and scribbled music onto the tablecloth. And Tchaikovsky, who drowned himself. And Hank Williams. They suffered. Did Akira? I wondered if Akira had had a normal childhood. Had he been good in school or just in music? When he walked around outside did he hear ordinary things differently? Could he read symphony scores as easily as books? Did he speak English? Was he lonely in a city where no one spoke Japanese?

From my bedroom window, I watched them unload his furniture. He didn't seem to have very much. The next morning his car, a white Camaro, was parked in the driveway.

I waited a week so he could get settled. Then I got too nervous thinking about seeing him so I waited another week. Then he left town on tour and another week went by.

I watched for lights in his house.

He was back.

I needed an excuse, something to take over, to meet him. My mother suggested brownies so I got up early and made two batches and then I made a third batch that was perfect so I cut each square out and arranged them in a tin that held its warmth as I carried it like a crèche down the street and up the flagstone steps of the house I still thought of as the Bennetts'.

I rang the bell.

My heart: my heart: my heart.

The door swung open and there was His Face. Huge, up close. I said hello and he smiled and bowed.

He waved me inside. His Japanese voice asked me to take off my shoes and he pointed to slippers inside the door. He took the brownies from my hand and then my coat and I felt big and awkward leaning down to undo my shoelaces while he watched. I was self-conscious about the size of my feet at that age. I hoped my socks were clean. The slippers he offered me looked so small. He was wearing a kimono. It was open at the throat and oh, his hair against the skin on his neck! Skin the colour of his voice asking me would I like tea and I nodded and was left standing alone in a room furnished Japanese-style, with cushions on the floor. No chairs. There was a low, black table, a white rug, eucalyptus branches in a vase by the fireplace which gave off a curious smell. A memory.

He came back with a tray and my opened tin of brownies on it, two tea cups and a pot. He sat cross-legged at the table and I copied him. I stared at his hair which was mixed in with strands of premature grey. His hair was wet-black and glossy; it trembled when he spoke, springing like a fountain from the crown of his head and spilling into his eyes. His eyes rolled up to meet mine, suddenly, and my scalp broke out in quills. His eyes were unlike anything I had ever seen before. Absolutely animal-shaped. We talked but I remember only a deafening pressure in my ears, my dry throat, his funny voice. I pulled everything in through my eyes – except his voice, creaky-gravelly, but also a bit feminine somehow. There was a strong Japanese tint to his words, to the way he repeated my name as he handed me my teacup. Em-mah. As though he was learning it by ear, like a bird.

We stood up. He invited me to return. He definitely did say to come back. The click of the door behind me played over and over as I floated back down his steps. Em-mah. How soon could I come back?

I walked up and down my street until I'd replayed every detail of the visit. Combed through it as though he was a dream I had to recall before the waking world tore it to shreds. I arrived back home and my parents fell on me. What was he like? I told them about his kimono and the slippers and how we'd had Japanese tea and how his furniture was totally different from the Bennetts'. I didn't tell them that already I missed him. That everything around me in my own house had suddenly faded into black and white.

That night, before I got into bed, I looked out my bedroom window at his house. His kitchen light was on. Maybe he was making tea. Maybe he was eating my brownies.

He began appearing in the papers all the time. He was photographed at formal receptions, shaking hands with soloists and symphony personnel. I clipped everything I saw. I cut out his picture and biography from the symphony programme. I carried a photo of him in my wallet. I thrilled myself imagining the ambulance driver discovering it after I'd thrown myself in front of Akira's car. I taped his picture to the dresser beside my bed so I'd wake up in the morning gazing into his face. I knew his Camaro by the sound of the engine as it came wheeling around the corner on the way out to rehearsal. I bought a ticket to his next concert and stared at him the whole time from the gallery rail. When my parents asked what had been played and who were the soloists, I'd forgotten completely and had to look everything up again in the programme.

I began to keep a window log.

Saturday.
   8:55 a.m. Akira out. Wearing sheepskin coat (gorgeous). Carrying briefcase.
   Noon: returned with case of American beer & laundry. Looks like tails.
   8:30 p.m. out. Sheepskin again. Missed return.
   11:15: all lights out.

One night, a few weeks after my brownie visit, I decided to try and get backstage. A suitable length of time had elapsed for me not to seem over-eager but I didn't want the brownies to wear off altogether, as it were. If he failed to recognize me, I promised myself I'd forget all about him.

The second I walked through the backstage door I knew I'd made a dreadful mistake. I was going to make a fool of myself. I was going to trip on something, revolt him somehow. This was the wrong time to come.

I had to find a washroom and comb my hair again,

get composed. I turned to get back out before anyone saw me when, suddenly at the end of another hall, I caught a glimpse of an indigo kimono, camelia pattern, white petals across his shoulders. It was him. Akira! And someone else. Oh my god. Coming towards me. His wet face. Wet hair. I flattened myself against the wall.

Em-mah! he cried and seized my hand, his face shining. Em-mah. You come to see me? You enjoy concert tonight? You must meet Manager. Manager, this is neigh-bah. Young girl who made me ahhh – Em-mah, what you call dis ting?

My voice creaked. Brownies, Akira.

Ahhh. Brrrrownies. He rolled his Rs operatically. Yes. Nice young lady, eh?

Manager nodded.

I could read the distaste in his mouth. He looked like José Ferrer, the scowling director in my favourite movie, *Enter Laughing*.

You must want to get dressed, Akira. I'll tell Heinz to bring your car around.

I was in the way. A nuisance to Manager. To Akira. My heart was pounding so hard. I was sure he could hear it. I was making a fool of myself. My ridiculous feelings were written all over my face. Stupid face. Idiot me.

Akira, I'll say goodbye now. See you soon.

No – wait! I drive you home, no? We ah neigh-bahs. You have time to wait for me?

I had time, yes. I nodded. He undid my hand. He was actually asking me to wait. He remembered me. He–.

Wasn't that a tiny dab of sauce on Manager's tie?

We pulled into his driveway and he invited me in. He held open the door, waiting, and I slipped past him without touching. He handed me a glass without touching. I said something funny and he laughed, his hand rocking my shoulder but there was air between his hand and the cloth, between his skin and mine. I inhaled the scent of his hair. What was happening to me? Why me? Don't break this glass, don't spill something, for god's sake. My legs are asleep. I just know I'm going to fall over if I stand up. Am I me, Emma, sitting here right now? Why do I have such a silly little nose. Oh please don't make me have to eat something in front of him. Just move that foot a little. Ahhh.

We finished tea, then he sagged with sudden fatigue and I shot to my feet, shook hands goodnight and flew down his steps and back home, to my room, my sanctum, to lie down and recall every last molecule of our encounter. The next few days, I sat through my classes like a zombie. Akira. Akira. Akira.

I am walking down the magic sidewalk.

A car pulled up beside me. Akira rolled down the window.

Hello, Emma. You are coming home from school? Maybe you see concert tonight. Not too much homework to do, I hope? You check with your parents, okay?

I nodded and shifted my books onto my hip. No homework, Akira. He drove off. Oh god, my skirt had been all hiked up sideways the whole time he'd been talking.

★

I began to go to all his concerts. He reserved complimentary tickets for me under his name at the box office. My parents asked me to thank him. They were embarrassed by such generosity. They asked me, was I making a nuisance of myself? Sometimes Akira drove us both there if I called at his house early. Often we drove back together. Or sometimes out to a restaurant to eat. He always conducted on an empty stomach.

I worked on my hair, my posture. I tried to dress better. My schoolwork began to slide. I inhaled the scent of everything Japanese that could tell me something more about him. I stole hairs from his hairbrush, Tokyo cigarettes from the package he left on the table when he went to answer the phone. I took a restaurant drinking-glass, faintly imprinted with his lips, and kept it in my top drawer. The last minutes of every visit with him pulled themselves through my clenched

31

fingers, bead by bead. He stood up to say goodbye one night and his cheek brushed mine.

Monday.
   6 p.m.: Akira returned from rehearsal. Blue ski-jacket. Carrying score.
   7 p.m.: Left. Dinner?
   10:45: Lights all out.

Everything Japanese became magic. Sheepskin coats were magic. I'd spot a car like his and my heart would jump. In the grocery store, I heard a laugh just like his and I almost died. I wanted to be like him, to feel perfect. Everything that connected to him was absolutely sacred. My daily life was so ordinary it was painful. I made notes after every encounter with Akira for fear I'd forget a detail. Sometimes other details from my ordinary life found their way in. They helped to define the days in my mind.

Wednesday.
   Akira reads his magazines from right to left. Sometimes down the page in columns. This must make a difference. But how?
   Marjorie crashed into my locker today. Asked me did I want a blind date tomorrow. Her brother's

friend. Finally, at mid-fourteen, I have been offered a d.a.t.e. (Log, take note.) But concert tomorrow night. Told Marjorie, sorry, I had to babysit. She insisted I was suicidal to turn him down he's in grade 13, at St. Mike's. I'll never get another chance. Only 27 more hours before Akira!! Maybe go backstage. Yippee. Note: Stand up straight. Borrow silk scarf from Mom.

10 p.m.: Car in driveway.

11:30: Lights out.

Saturday

It worked! I stood at the top of the street, timed it, began to stroll down the hill just when I thought he'd be coming around the corner back from rehearsal. A few false starts. Then this time, for real. He saw me before I saw him, pulled up beside me, rolled down the window (black turtleneck) and invited me back for tea. Love sitting beside him, watching his hands drive.

Tuesday

Was invited by Louise and Tricia (the superhip twins) to go jam-can curling. Grossed them out by turning up with skates. But they told me it was on ice!

Akira can't digest cheese. Too heavy, he said, patting his belly. He was brought up on soy milk, not cow's milk. Oh, my mother said, he doesn't have our enzymes.

Another fact to add to my secret book of differences.

Thursday
Dream night. Saw A. backstage after. Face covered in sweat. Blue flowered kimono again. Looked the best! Touched my hand when introducing me to pianist! Manager insisted they go out to a bar afterwards. I had to leave. Bummer. Hate mgr. Guy knows it's a school night plus I'm underage. Akira seemed sorry. My imag.?

Wednesday
No concert until Tues. Fainted in health class today. A vd film and the animation was so *real* I stood up and blacked out. Now everyone will think I have IT. Marj told me my eyes actually rolled back into my head. So embarrassing. My kilt flipped up too, she said. She brought my books around to the nurse's office. Later. M. insists Seth wants to meet me. She says hang out in the schoolyard at St. Mike's after class. But A. comes back from rehearsal 4:30-ish. Can't tell Marj. about A. yet. Wish I wasn't so much taller now than A.

Saturday

The language. He laughed when I told him my brownies tasted better than they looked. That was funny? But he completely missed my ironic jokes and when I exaggerated to be funny, he just looked blank. He laughed today when the tuba player lumbered off-stage like a grizzly bear during rehearsal. He loves slapstick. I'm embarrassed. In other ways he seems so much more sophisticated than anyone I've ever met.

Sunday

2-4 p.m. Saw A. pacing to music out on his balcony. Could hear actual sound of his humming over the music. Turn fifteen next month.

Wednesday.

A. on tour for a month. What a birthday present. Folks tried to cheer me up in time for my party. How am I going to survive. Virginia Rickler showed me the strychnine rings in her hair from the bad acid she's taken. Claims she can date the trips from the rings. Good thing her parents are still in Brazil. Heard also that Carole Lasker's brother flipped out and drove off Gorse Hill on his bike. They didn't find him for hours and now they think permanent brain damage ... Carole can't stand anyone who does drugs now.

Friday

Chandeliers versus paper lanterns. Wallpaper, any wallpaper, versus shoji screens. Coffee versus green tea. Black oxfords versus zoris. A Victorian chesterfield, for god's sake, versus floor cushions. Steak-and -kidney pie versus sushi. We westerners wear our hair in frizzy balls, stick our arms into tight sleeves that catch rings of perspiration, clump and glop our way across the outdoors, couldn't tell you three things about the changing seasons, use up entire rooms with four-poster beds. It takes us two miles to turn around. We have amnesia too. Japanese household traditions date back hundreds of years. I can't remember what day Hallowe'en falls on or trace anything through our European hodge podge. I couldn't memorize a recipe to save my life.

Friday

Formal is coming. Gaahhh. Can't duck out. A. on tour again helps. Marj & Lynn insist on total mutual makeovers. Glad I finally told them about A. Hated lying, complications etc. They think I should try and meet boys, somebody, anybody, in time for formal. Why should I? Am I normal? Dear log, am I normal?

Saturday

Noon: A. leaves house.

2 p.m.: Returns. A. got haircut!! (Find out where)

5:30: Leaves. Carrying laundry. Glimpse of red turtleneck.

– missed return.

11:45: lights out.

Wednesday

Manners. Oh, manners. Akira eats noisily, talks with his mouth full, drops food from his chopsticks into the sauce. But in the car today he sneezed and apologized, embarrassed as though he'd farted. On most occasions his attentiveness to other people is so much subtler than mine, I feel ashamed – thinking of how 'my people' clump around with their boots on in the house, sit in dirty bathwater, wear streetclothes until bedtime, interrupt one another, drag a tree into the house or hack a face out of a pumpkin to celebrate a season, saw our meat up and stab it, laugh *haw haw haw*. We're cowhands!

They don't call it the other side of the world for nothing. In Japan, everything must be different.

Makeover a total failure. Tried wearing the headband home after school today. People actually snickered. God I hate people my age. M. took me aside, told me my forehead too low for a headband. Looks goofy with my uniform. Formal is getting closer. A total put-through! I hate every speck of my life except A.

11 p.m. kitchen light goes out.

37

Tuesday

The Japanese probably have to recycle much more than we do. Every object is precious, hard to replace. Food is arranged in individual bitefuls – not like the pails of carrots, mashed potatoes and turkey I turned out into serving bowls last night and scraped later into a heap of bones and sludge that was lugged out to the street in a plastic bag. Our backyard is a shaggy-edged bowl of shade slashed with the fountain scar, old bicycle parts and snow tires.

Friday

Blind date's car comes in twenty minutes. So nervous. I am not right for this dress it's way too weird across the boobs I told Marj it was ridic. Why does she bully me. These shoes put me over six feet. God almighty. Why couldn't I go in my kimono? With A. Wish it was next week and he was home. Wish I was Maria Callas. Uh oh. Doorbell. Glad A. can't see me looking like this. I kiss your picture Akira. Quick, give me courage.

Saturday

Seth. At first he wouldn't talk. I hate shrimp cocktail. In those tricky little glasses I knew I'd spill mine. Lucky my skirt was black. The cummerbund (like Akira's) is ruined though. No one else was wearing blouses and skirts, just backless, strapless. Hair up in buns, pierced ears. I couldn't find heels in size eleven. I looked like a baby, nothing to push up, pink lipstick and everyone else wearing red. Seth danced so close I could feel everything and they must have had liquor in the washroom how else could he have gotten so drunk. In the parking lot I had to hold his tails back so he could barf. Then he tried to French-kiss me. Marj says give him another chance. I told her she's on probation setting me up like that.

Monday

Japanese objects all seem to be made as small as possible, easily taken apart and put away. I love the idea of growing miniature trees, raking gravel into patterns, pushing six square feet of dirt into a dream garden.

Turned fifteen today. Akira is thirty-seven. I am still growing. We stood back to back and looked in the mirror. I positively tower over him now. We both burst out laughing. Actually Akira doesn't laugh. He only smiles open-mouthed and very occasionally makes a kind of *ha* noise. Only one.

Fifteen. Still no blood. In a class by myself. That's it, I thought. I'm barren. A tiny thrill of hope. No blood ever.

My parents were getting irritated with my infatuation. I should be dating boys, they protested, while I sawed the legs off my bed and my dresser and took to eating on the floor. I drank milk from a *sake* carafe, ate Christmas dinner with chopsticks, spent my clothing allowance on Japanese language records, imitated Akira's voice, walked like him, conducted like him in the mirror. He brought me back a summer cotton kimono from Tokyo which I wore bunched up under my uniform. My mother discovered my shrine of keepsakes. Disgusted, she flushed his hair down the toilet and washed out the drinking-glass. I flew into a rage and cried for two days. I hid the cigarettes, the ticket stubs, the dressing-room towel he'd wiped his face on. My father used a Japanese accent to get my attention and howled on all fours when I put on my Kabuki record.

Akira asked me about school and tried to recall what fifteen had been like for him. We stood back-to-back. I pressed down his hair. He pressed his spine against mine. We touched together, from the shoulder blades down to our heels. I was three and a half inches taller than him now. He made a joke – he was shrinking! He told me everything about himself. His English was never a problem. The heat he produced in me could have fogged film, yet it was uninformed, inert. I discuss everything with Emma, – Akira said proudly to Manager – except sex. *Our love is special*.

First Blood. Suddenly when I stood up. Blood on my kilt, on my chair, in my sock.

I turned sixteen looking at myself sideways in the mirror. I still screamed androgyny.

Our glasses clinked and Akira tousled my hair. Called himself an old man. I protested – no! – but he laughed and looked away.

He lifted his cup. This is Buddha. He touched the table. This is Buddha. Everything has Buddha nature inside. We believe God is not up there, he pointed. But here. He touched his nose.

We believe. I shivered. So much separated us.

★

I knew she was going to get me. I could just feel it in my bones, even before I walked into the gym. I felt conspicuous. It was time. She'd ignored me for almost a month. She was clairvoyant. She'd know I was thinking these thoughts. She'd get me for sure.

I rolled back the elastic on the legs of my bloomers. It was so tight it cut off the circulation in my legs. I hated how I looked in them. Other girls looked so much better ...

Emma! Over here.

I walked over to her.

Unroll that elastic. You look ridiculous.

I did as I was told.

What are we supposed to be doing today?

Handstands.

What?

Handstands, Miss Pike.

Show me.

I threw my hands down and jumped up. Not high enough. I bucked again. Not high enough.

And what do you call those?

Silence. She couldn't get me if I was silent.

Class! Gather around.

Filthy bitch. She was Stalag Nine. She was Helga the She-wolf. I wanted to rip out her tongue.

Emma. Get up and DO IT PROPERLY!

I admit it. I was a total coward, afraid of crashing, breaking my spine and spending the rest of my life in a wheelchair.

I bucked again. The change cascaded out of my shirt pocket.

What in heaven's name is that?

Akira's photo. Ohmygod. I'd forgotten. There was his face, inches from my own, in full view of everyone, baton raised in hand. Shitshitshit. Akira. Get out of here.

I focused on his face, threw my hands down again, heaved my hips up over my head, straightened my back and wobbled there, for a few seconds, the blood pounding behind my eyes. Akira. Save us. Get us out of this.

The whistle blew.

Again!

I heaved myself up once again, managed to straighten my back without going over, pointed my toes the way I was supposed to, hung there, squashing the grit into my palms, my shirt, untucked now and sliding up my chest. Oh god, now they'll see I don't wear a bra.

She blew the whistle. I came down.

Onto my own hands. I don't know how it happened but those were my running shoes all right with my fingers sticking out underneath them and I couldn't pull out, or lift off or step back. I just squatted on top of myself, my eyes fuzzing over. It seemed ages until I solved it suddenly, crashed down onto my side and popped my hands out, all purple with tread-marks and then, with a jerk, I got up again, almost blacked out doing it so fast, started stuffing my shirt back in and gathering up my change and Akira's photo, afraid to look at Pike for fear the look on my face would show her how much I – IMPUDENCE, she'd bellow at me – but she didn't. She flashed me a little smile instead, much more disturbing, and lurched away.

The rest of the class wheeled back to their places and began to practise like little gazelles, safe now, while the glutted lion prowled amongst them.

I retreated to my regular corner, under the ropes.

The whole class knew I was the ultimate geek. I didn't care. The moment this period was over, I was going home to get changed. To see Akira tonight. And afterwards I would probably go back to his house for tea. Or out for Chinese food. While these people watched tv. Or yakked on the phone with boys or washed their hair. I looked down at my hands. Magic hands! They'd touched Akira ! They'd been to his house.

★

Akira got sick. He complained of winds, of dampness inside. He wrapped a scarf around his belly to keep warm but left his shirt open. The *hara*, three fingers below the navel, was a magic place. The body's furnace. Courage and balance were hidden there. The suicide spot.

I walked to school along cracks, seams, the tops of walls, thinking, *hara, hara*. Breathing from the navel. I swear it was easy – for the first time, I balanced!

★

Moon Viewing

I began reading prison books – in which the heroine escapes her captors by molding a dummy of herself out of bedclothes and soap slivers, is shipwrecked, rations a crust of bread over five days, wrings water out of a raw fish caught with an earring. Books about fugitives, castaways bobbing on the Pacific and punitive private schools changed the taste of soup and bread for me forever.

Rationing the everyday things in life gave them magic. Japanese magic.

I closed my book, leaned on my elbows and looked down at Akira's house. The blizzard had almost covered the dark roof. Yellow light leaked out from his bedroom window onto the snowy balcony. His roof looked so close I could almost reach through the trees and snap off a piece like candy.

It looked like a medicine chest only deeper and it was mounted on the living-room wall. When Akira left the room to make a phone-call one day, I got my chance. One ear cocked, I cautiously pulled the double doors ajar. Was the box firmly attached? *A bang, crash. Emma on the floor surrounded by box splinters. Akira's look!* I squinted into the back of the box. I could just make out the photograph of an old man. Akira's father? There was an incense holder, a tiny scroll, some matches. *I am peering into Akira's secret heart.*

Akira was still on the phone. Beside the photo – a statue of the Buddha and a tiny plate with a *sake* cup and a tangerine on it. What prayers did Akira offer? I closed my eyes, breathed in the faintly jasmined air of the shrine box, visualizing Akira in mysterious, ceremonial clothes.

Akira hung up. I closed up the box and raced back onto my cushion, heart pounding.

He walked in. It's snowing in Berlin, he said. Can you believe it, this time of year? Snow in Berlin!

★

Don't let a policeman come, he said. I'll just be a minute. He dashed out of the car and across the street to a Japanese grocery store. So this was where he

46

bought his food. I made a mental note of the address. I'd have to come back and investigate. The minutes passed.

I couldn't help it. I punched open the glove compartment and the contents exploded onto the floor. Oh god. I began stuffing things back in, receipts for gas (his autograph on every one!) a package of Japanese candy, winter gloves, an electric shaver, a mini-bottle of whiskey, the kind you get on airplanes. I shook a candy into my hand and squashed the door shut on the rest of the stuff. I kept the wrapper for my archives and popped the candy into my mouth. It was gum! Instantly I reeked of an odd, unrecognisable fruit flavour. The whole car reeked. I looked up and it was too late to swallow – Akira was walking back, his arms full of groceries. I pushed the door open for him and the moment he sat down he sniffed and looked at me, the wrapper still in my hand. Ahhh, so you find my gum, he said, a little smile playing across his face.

Unusual taste, I managed, once my blush had faded. *And now I am a total joke to him. How long has he known ... about me?*

Spring arrived.

I finished my tea and then Akira broke the news that he had accepted a new job, as conductor and music director of an orchestra in Europe. He was moving on.

Last evening.

We sat on the floor of his empty house and talked about the year ahead and toasted his European orchestra. I twisted my glass around on its napkin at the low table watching Akira tug cigarette smoke down into his throat then gracefully exhale it through his nose in a way I found so Japanese. He rolled his eyes up to me and tilted his head away.

I stood at the door and he gathered me into his arms – I could feel our hearts through the cloth – I told him I loved him but he pressed us together – please no talking. And this moment – like all the others – was being pulled away from me, bead by bead.

I was watching Akira mount the podium, he was ordering from the waiter. The car pulled away with his face in the window. I bowed goodbye and stepped backward. The audience rose with a roar as he bowed again. The phone rang. It was San Francisco. It was raining and we were running hand in hand for a taxi, his face came close as we stepped in and he apologised. He lifted the needle from the record and turned to refill our teacups. I repeated his name to the woman at the ticket window, shouting this time, and her eyebrows flew up. Applause was cutting into the first bars as I crawled across people's knees. I was dashing across the street after his car. I was flying towards his dressing room. He was whispering into Manager's ear with his eyes on me. I nodded formally, turning to catch a smile from him. The scowling soloist held out a hand. There was a rustle of tails as he passed. Akira was crooning the theme as he turned the pages of his score, asking me to stay while he studied. I passed him his cigarette. It was long distance again. He closed his eyes as he listened and rocked, cross-legged. I was lifted up with the crowd and swept through the foyer where I lost him. I spotted his hair, he waved me through and we ran backstage to his room. The baton clicked inside its case, he threw his tails across the back seat. Snowing again. His face wet. Someone handed him a towel. His baton clicked against the edge of the podium. Airplane tickets were splayed behind the mirror. His flight was delayed: we had two hours more. Flowers were pushed through the dressing room door. I read him the name aloud. His sweat flew in a spray off his hair which the camera lens picked up. I stood at the foot of the stairs. He looked down and grinned. We stood back-to-back. His animal-shaped eyes locked with mine, his golden hand closed over my own. His eyes clouded over with fatigue. He pushed his hair back. The applause faded.

The last seconds ticked away until suddenly there was no more time between us. I counted my heart: Ten. Nine. Eight. Seven. Six. Five. Four. Three. Two. One.

Curtain call.

I don't care about anything I just want him back I don't want to talk to anybody I don't want to go to school no one understands I don't want to get up I can't lie down I can't sleep AKIRA! I just want him back again. I can't eat I want him to come back no one understands – they think – but if I could hear his voice again hear him talk hear that car coming around the corner again I'm a good person why did this no there's no one I need to talk to please come back Akira please I'm dying please come back –

Nothing will bring him back.

It wasn't premeditated – except for the bangs.

I spread out newspapers under the chair by the bathroom mirror. Snip, snip and then I saw I should have wet my hair first. I'd taken the front off too high on the left. So I corrected that but then the sides looked really goofy. I was thinking about Akira and being obsessed by his empty house. He'd been gone a week now. Life went on like normal at school. I wasn't a widow – I wasn't Jackie Kennedy – what was I? My parents acted like, whew, thank heavens things can get back to normal around here. Stop yer mooning. Get outside and blow the stink off you. What I call their Ozark routine. I wasn't on speaking terms with them. Maybe I was trying to get back at them. Anyway, I tried to correct what I'd done with the front and sides but every curl that popped up and got nicked off with the nail scissors made it worse and, you can imagine, I started running out of hair. Both ears showed and I was getting bugged by the back – couldn't get at it properly and then I thought, what the hell. I'll just take the whole thing off and start again. Hair grows back. It'll be a deadline for my mourning. I was thinking along those lines, honestly. At a half an inch or so a month, I'll be back to normal in a year. Sort of. That's when I thought of using the razor. I got my hair down to a stubble using the scissors and then I wet what was left and put on lather – at this point I was totally into the transformation; there was nowhere else to go, hairwise. That first drag of the razor made me so nervous.

So noisy too, close to the skull like that. I started cutting myself when the skin rolled – little tufts of hair with cuts in the furrows – until I figured out how to pull my scalp taut first. Amazing how puffy the skin is there, like a cushion. And so grey. I cut myself a few more times and then I remembered Dad's styptic pencil. It stung like a wasp.

I was starting in to shave the back when I heard my parents come in the front door. My schoolbag was sitting on the hall chair.

They might come upstairs. They might not. I put the razor down in my lap and waited.

Before skull and bones? You were this. You were the dust blowing around the corner.

I came back but ... eggs under the skin had hatched into worms that stitched their way towards my heart. They had an appetite of their own. They fed on japonica.

A hunter drops a ball of blubber every few yards, baited with a coiled spring of whalebone, harpoon-tipped. The bear follows, eating them. As the blubber dissolves, barb after barb springs open inside its belly.

A wolf licks the frozen carcass carefully baited with razors. Frenzied by the taste of blood on its own slashed tongue, it licks faster and faster.

Hyakumi — various delicacies offered to the dead.

Tools of enlightenment

A tile shatters against a tree.
A dog throws itself against the gate.
A drop lands on the newspaper with a pat.
A photo flutters from a pocket.
Sweat flies off in a spray.
A voice gives a ha laugh.
A baton clicks inside its case.
A car slows to a crawl behind me.
A handful of hair floats to the floor.

Even a sardine's head can become an object of worship if one has faith.   SHINRAN

Marjorie riffled my stubble with her palm. Ooh. What a feeling. The ultimate easy-care cut. She bent over, giggled into my face. I'd never have the guts to do that. It IS growing back though. But when I heard, I was afraid maybe …

I'd be stuck bald forever?

Well, no. Of course not. Do you feel okay now? I mean are you still obsessed with him? How are you going to explain this at school? Your face looks so round! She tugged my hair. Whispered into it, growgrowgrow.

They'll think I had an operation. They'll be afraid to ask. Here's my plan. I finish grade thirteen. I get a job. I save up and as soon as I've got two thousand dollars together, voom – Japan. Who knows? Akira's there every year. Maybe I'll look him up.

And live happily ever after? Emma, are you for real?

Ah come on, Marjorie. I just want to see the guy again. That's all. Why are you looking at me like that?

Maybe it's the hair. You looked crazy there for a second.

Girl talk.

It was August.

My parents came down from the cottage to get me. They'd bought me a present – a red canvas canoe with honey-coloured ribs, so light I could carry it myself. They wanted me to invite a school-friend up too but I was out of touch with everyone by now. So the three of us strapped the canoe to the roof of the car along with a month's worth of baggage and food, and drove out of town.

I couldn't wait to take long solo paddles along the shores of the lake. One calm day I paddled all the way into town, pulled the canoe up on shore and went shopping, piled the groceries into the belly of the canoe and was back in time for lunch.

There was outdoor work to do, which I liked. We tore the old boathouse down, pulled out deadheads and cut them up with the Swede saw, took garbage to the dump.

My birthday, end of August, was a make-work project I would happily have skipped this year but my mother hated to break with tradition. It was an excuse to round up our fellow cottagers, most of whom had kids far too young for me, and have a party. My mother dreamed up themes every year. We had done animals, signs of the zodiac, heroes and villains, TV characters. This year, because so many of the kids were little, she chose vegetables.

We crayoned onions and broccolis on the table napkins, made a vegetable-people table centre, a zucchini canoe with carrot ladies and pickle gentlemen who paddled across a shaving-mirror lake. My father made himself a lei of Brussels sprouts. My mother bustled around me with broccoli buds behind each ear, pinning Queen Anne's Lace (a relative of the wild carrot) around my head. She was still unhappy about my hair of course, but by now the scalp was completely hidden. We all looked ridiculous today. The ritual, the repetitiveness of it, the notion of birthdays itself, of being given token presents by strangers, of having to laugh and act the centrepiece, of going through the motions of celebrating – I shuddered. Empty. Meaningless. But I'd put my parents through so much, I wanted to make amends if I could.

Families began to arrive. Motorboats loaded to the gunwales zoomed up to the dock and swamped it with backwash, and then everybody jumped out, tipping the floating dock and kids screamed and fell in, their party clothes ballooning up under their life-jackets. The kids were rescued, presents retrieved, shoes wrung out, vegetable crowns retied and then it was up the hill to the barbecue where my father officiated, leering over his Brussels sprouts at the tiniest kids until they shrieked in fright and fell over. Hot-dogs covered in grit.

I stumbled detachedly through the day like a sleepwalker, in spite of my efforts to partake. The expression current among my peers was: Unreal. And it was.

Adults took me aside, stared into my hair, asked me

again how old I was this year and, to a one, declared how lucky I was. Eighteen! The oyster of the world opening before my very eyes. My wonderful youth, etc. Everything before me. I felt a thousand years old, infinitely tired. A horrible logic inside told me that the best years of my life had just ended.

Silence was yelled for. It was time to read my horoscope, another tradition. My father handed me the tiny pink drugstore scroll. I took a swallow of orange crush and began to read aloud:

'Until the 29th, you will be very much preoccupied with personal and private issues. It is apparent that one partnership, involvement, or association has run its course and work is definitely your best therapy now. However a great deal depends on whether you are willing to forget what has overshadowed you in the past.'

My throat constricted.

'If attachment has to be terminated it should be without a feeling of despondency. Even though the sun is passing through Gemini at a decidedly adverse angle to Jupiter you appear to be entering a decisive period.'

(A banging of knives and spoons.)

'You are simply cutting out the dead wood in your life in preparation for a more constructive phase. '

(My mother in a stage whisper: I can think of some dead wood around here that needs cutting ...)

'Shhh, Mom.' (Pause.) 'You will be able to decide on the right course of action and see situations in their true perspective soon. The truth of these statements will be supported by developments around the time the Sun opposes Uranus, on the 30th. Be patient.'

(A toast was proclaimed: To the new moon! To the new moon!)

I rolled up the scroll and hid it in my shirt. The cake came and I made a wish, the usual, impossible wish I'd made every day since Akira left. But as I thought it and blew out the candles to another year I also hoped, for the first time, that this thing inside me would move on.

I passed a florist's shop when the smell hit me – eucalyptus. Instantly, I was transported back to his room, to the low table, floor cushions, split in two colours of silk, the colours of Kabuki theatre, he told me once. The red tiles of his fireplace and the vase of branches in it. The oily smell released from a leaf crushed between his fingers as he talked.

I walked into the store. Branches of eucalyptus lay heaped in baskets on the floor. I crushed a leaf and out came that smell. I bought a huge armful, transformed myself into a walking Sumi-e brush trailing an inky perfume through the shoppers, down into the subway, jostling the crowd every way I turned. The bundle crushed against me as I rode the train across town, the smell so strong now, it was medicinal. Bringing him back to me through a lens of oil – the details released, a few atoms at a time. Akira's cushions, the thready silk, his hand reaching behind him for a branch, his flat nails, the fine gold chain around his neck – the train jerked me home, crushing him against me again and again.

★

In my dream, I am in a shoestore. There has been a sale and chairs and boxes are scattered about. Exhausted saleswomen doze against a stack of inventory.

A pair of rubber boots sits on a chair, very tall and decorated across the toe with a curious red pattern I recognise as Japanese. Delighted, I grab it and instantly the red pattern slides off. It is only a ribbon which has drifted down from the ceiling. Still, I want a pair for myself and begin rummaging around among the boxes looking for my size but the characters are all written in Japanese. I empty the boxes out onto the floor searching for a pair to fit me but each boot I pick up is smaller than the last. No bigger than the palm of my hand.

The situation persists into the next day like a weird drugstore perfume.

★

I tracked down Akira's Japanese grocery store in Chinatown and went in. Foodstuffs coiled as neatly as hair or bound around like firewood or shaped into little bricks and folded in half like wallets. Bundles of leaves that turned like the pages of a book and swelled ten times their size, in hot water. Speckled clothesline in tight bladders of water, human ears threaded on strings, fish ground into pink mud, roe like vitamin capsules. Seaweed spirals to be ground into powder and sprinkled over rice. One-sided fish shining through their packages like Polaroid photographs.

The tin of wasabi. Two inches high, decorated with a vivid lithograph of mountains, a rainbow, a swollen river and fluorescent green radishes thrown onto the bank. The calligraphy soared out of a brilliant sky, obliterating nothing behind it.

Objects of worship.

Vive la difference, the shelves whispered. And after a while, *Live the difference* and finally, *Leave the difference, leave the difference.*

After I graduated, I asked for a job there and got it.

The man put his purchase on the counter. Smiled at me. He was very handsome. Tall for a Japanese.

'Matsutake mushrooms very expensive,' he noted, as I dropped them on the scale.

'A little, but they're so good,' I said, smiling back. 'That'll be twelve dollars.'

He gasped and clapped his hand across his heart. Reached for his wallet.

'Are you going to cook these yourself?' I asked.

He smiled. 'Of course. I am bachelor.' Slight accent. He looked to be in his mid-twenties. Playful eyes. 'You must know all about Japanese food, yes? You have worked here long?'

I gave him his change. Wrapped up his mushrooms. His fingernails looked like Akira's.

'Two years.'

He put his wallet away but hesitated. 'My name is Masaaki – Mas, for short. May I ask your name?'

'Emma.'

'Bye bye, Missis Emma.'

'Bye Mister Masaaki.'

His eyes twinkled.

Next week he was back.

'Konichi-wah, Missis Emma. Good afternoon.'

I nodded. His hand rested on his purchases. I reached for them and his hand touched mine. When I gave him back his change our hands touched again.

'Working hard, Missis Emma?'

He was watching my face as I wrapped his packages. 'You are doing very good job. Onions are quite safe now, I think.'

I looked down and blushed. I had wrapped each one separately in newspaper.

He picked up his bags and left. For the rest of the day, I squirmed a little each time I remembered him. He must have thought I was a complete –

I locked the till, turned off the lights, set the alarm and slammed the door behind me. Went over to my bicycle and began undoing the combination lock.

'Missis Emma.'

I jumped. He stepped out of the shadows.

'Please. Sorry to surprise you. I would like to invite you somewhere. For a beer perhaps, or coffee?'

'Well, I … '

'Please? He put his hand on my bicycle seat. It's very hot day. You need a beer after hard work all day long.'

He was a foreign student at the University of Toronto, it turned out, doing graduate studies in computer science. He was twenty-six, lived in a rooming house in the Annex, on a scholarship and had another year to go before he returned to take up his career with a Tokyo corporation. His English was excellent except for his articles. Better than Akira's. He was almost six feet, slight shoulders, long limbs, short hair.

We began to go out. He picked me up in his car, always coming in first to say hello to my parents who were duly impressed with his tie and jacket. He always brought me home at a decent hour and we did old-fashioned things like picnics, trips to the zoo, the museum, the art gallery. Dinners in restaurants. He never took me back to his apartment or suggested anything improper. A perfect gentleman.

But I told Marjorie the truth. That almost from the very first, his hand lingered on my back, my ass, in public places, that the moment his station wagon turned the corner he was leaning over to kiss me, his tongue in my mouth, one hand fumbling to open my blouse. That we never socialized with one another's friends. That the zoo was really the country where, in the shadow of the car, we spread out a rug and rolled over and over, fumbling, anxious, scared. He confessed that he was a virgin. He wanted to go inside. I was terrified of a single drop landing on me. Was positive I'd get pregnant if he touched me there for even an instant. Each time he began to get my skirt up, I bucked against his thigh, squeezed my legs together, wriggled below him until he groaned and slipped off.

In the wintertime, we threw our skates into the back seat but we never drove anywhere near a rink. Instead he took me to an underground garage – he was always discovering new hideaways – where we could lie together in the back of the wagon and neck until the windows steamed up. As his excitement mounted he would make a whimpering sound and then I knew I had to reach down for him, unwind the layers of clothing from around his nodding little stick of heat, barely longer and wider than my finger and work the skin up and down until his groans changed, steepened in pitch and his legs began to tremble uncontrollably, it was partly the cramped space, our nervousness, the naughtiness of it. But he never came. He made me use my mouth, pressing my head down until I gagged, the tears streaming but he still couldn't come and I couldn't come either although he loved to slide his slender fingers up my skirt until he found me and he had obviously been reading technique books – I could sense him turning the pages but I just couldn't let go. At first, I fantasized he was Akira, squinted my eyes and lost myself inside his hair. But how could this twitching man above me, with his pants open, have been Akira?

Making love to Akira wasn't what I wanted at all. My body proved that. And it was certainly not Masaaki I wanted either.

I wondered why he kept calling me up. Each time his car drove off, I figured that was the last I'd see of him. But the following week the phone would ring again. It got weirder. Between dates, Mas began to call and just breathe on the phone as soon as he heard my voice. He would breathe and then begin to whimper and I suddenly realized what he was doing. He whispered, Emma, Emma. And I would listen. Then interrupt in my daytime voice. Mas. Stop this. My folks are home. You're crazy. And he'd pant faster, faster.

We parked on a hill overlooking the city. I told him. Mas. This is not good. For either of us. You have to study. I can't do this any longer. I just can't. Find someone else. Maybe someone older.

He slid closer to me. Turned the headlights off. Please Emma. Just this once. Let me go inside. I promise I'll be careful. Just this once. Please please. His mouth was all over me. He reached down and undid his fly, pressed himself against me, whispering, You like it, you like it, I know you do, just let me come inside, give you pleasure – He was trembling, his movements more desperate, he pushed me back by the wrists, forced his knees between mine. I wrestled him, the door handle digging into my back, he was stronger than I thought. I brought one leg up but he kneed it down again and holding both my arms with one hand now, began tugging at my skirt with the other. Mas! I hissed. Quit this! You're being ridiculous. But his eyes glittered. My struggles were actually exciting him. I grabbed a fistful of hair and yanked his face off mine and he slapped me across the cheek and began to grind his hips against me.

You like it? It feels good? Can you feel me, Emma

how much I want you? Touch me. Touch me – and he twisted his penis out of his pants forced my hand down on it.

I slid my hip below him and jerked up.

He gasped and sagged off me, opened the car door and curled into a ball in the darkness beyond. Silence. Just the sound of his gagging. And the traffic wafting up from the city below.

Marjorie introduced me to him.

He was unlike Masaaki in every way although he too, was involved with computers. He was my age, he enjoyed socializing with my friends and he never, never pressured me into sex. He drove a motorcycle which was sexy but hardly a shagginwagon. With Boris I actually did go to the museum, the art gallery. He was mechanically adept and could cook. He loved puttering around the house with my father but was just as much at home in the kitchen talking food with my mother. My parents adored him in spite of the motorcycle.

★

'Boris,' I asked, as we picnicked on the hillside overlooking the Gardiner Expressway – our special spot, a stone's throw away from BurgerQueen, a dramatic spiral up from the Don Valley which made motorcycling down at sunset particularly terrific, in fact the same hill Masaaki had crumpled onto – 'what are your aspirations?'

Well, you know, a career in electronic engineering. Plus, I want stuff.'

'Stuff? What kind of stuff?'

'Well, stuff-stuff. You know. A house. A backyard. A skylight. Kids.'

'Oh my god, really?'

'There's stuff and there's *stuff*, Emma. I don't want

to hurt your feelings but a lot of the stuff around your house doesn't qualify. Hey, sun's going down, let's catch it!'

One afternoon, shortly after that, I felt I loved him and we went to bed together.

He went off to university but before he left, he insisted I needed a change. He couldn't bear the thought of me sticking out yet another year in my Japanese grocery store at six dollars an hour so he put out the word and a computer warehouse offered me something in inventory that paid considerably more.

It marked the beginning of the end of the person I'd been before meeting Boris. He worked like herbal medicine on my system — delicately at first but over time, a very potent drug. His value system gradually replaced my own, cell by cell, until the day came when it drew air on its own. Boris insisted that I had been *formless* in a way, all along, that I'd been a potato-person, full of potential that he'd shaped, whittled, seasoned and brought to maturity. He'd poked in cloves for eyes, pimento for a mouth. He'd peeled off lack of confidence, my yearnings to be someone I wasn't, my negative fascination with normalcy, my nostalgia for the years between fourteen and seventeen. The Akira years, as he called them, accounted for my ineffectual, noncompetitive, goal-less, vague, lumpy sensibility. 'Slough them off. They don't *work* for you any more,' Boris entreated me. A Kabuki doll was a lovely object to look at but I didn't want to be one. I accepted this. I let myself be whittled and refor-matted. I was eager to make myself over. I wanted to get on with life. I wanted to get over Akira.

A photograph from that time shows me wearing Boris' leather jacket astride his state-of-the-art Honda 650. I am squinting at Boris, looking a bit like my mom in that autumn light, Boris is standing beside me, smiling with a piston wrench in hand. Already there is something about his eyes. As though his self-absorption had sprouted leaves, blotting out the spon-taneous lights inside that had first attracted me to him.

★

Boris found a half-floor on Adelaide street, in what was listed as a 'mixed-use' area. You can't live at home forever, he said. Wait'll you see this space. We can fix it up exactly the way we want it. I stared through the slatted floorboards of the freight elevator lurching its way up to our loft.

He heaved the doors of our cage apart – they opened up like monster jaws instead of the other way on – Watch your step, Emma. Don't look down.

We went up onto the roof first. Our building was tucked behind a windshield factory, across the street from a car-wash. Lone men flitted in and out of the shadows below us. Not a tree in sight.

Boris took my hand and led me into the loft. It was the size of a dance studio. He talked fast, blocking out space with both arms. We'll put in a kitchen here, a shower here, partition this area off into working and living space. You can cook over here, we'll hang pots from that pipe over your head, you can watch the carwash, see the sun set from your stove, I'll be over here at my desk – he paced off the area – we'll put a loft bed in here, bolt it into this – he slapped the beam of wood sandwiched between layers of brick on the wall – a reading light, a roof garden, another work-cubicle at the other end, next to the shower-stall for you, if you'd like. And here – He waltzed into the middle of the room – is where we'll eat. And all the rest, his arms swirled, is unassigned space.

Unassigned space. *My* stove. Work cubicles. I felt uneasy.

I caught onto the knack of punching the stop-start buttons to jerk the cage in increments until it was flush with the loft level, sliding the cans out onto the landing then going back down for another load. I cleaned up and painted while Boris worked tirelessly from the blueprint in his head, sawing wood, drilling holes, stripping wire. The loft provided full expression for his perfectionism. He installed a shower stall, a sink, shelves above the stove, a platform bed with storage boxes suspended from strapping. For our wardrobe, he said. He was a bird in love, flitting about with string and twigs in his mouth, showing me what a good provider he was.

I suggested a low table on the floor, a tatami platform maybe, for serving tea on. Folding chairs without legs, for sitting around the table. A scroll alcove to break up the unassigned wall-space. A little juniper bush in a pot maybe. Everything as spare and light as possible. I'm not a Buddhist monk, Boris snorted. My legs can't take sitting on the floor. His heart was set on modular metal bookshelves, industrial light fixtures bolted overhead on rheostats, some oak furniture of his family's.

We'd been working for close to six weeks on the loft when we had our first serious fight.

I had expressed nervousness about enclosing the plumbing above the kitchen sink. In case we had to get at it later. I thought accoustic ceiling tiles were unnecessary and uninteresting –

How can you live looking up at pipes and naked rafters? Like we were goats in a barn, he snapped. You disturb me saying things like that, Emma. Just because you lived like a hillbilly in the past doesn't mean you –

I didn't grow up in a barn, Boris. What are you saying? And don't roll your eyes at me like that. You look demented.

Silence.

You want to squat on the floor, Emma. You want to live by candlelight and shuffle around in zoris. We can't ask our friends to do that. This is North America, Emma. You are North American. It's time you grew up and accepted that.

Exactly what are you saying, Boris?

But he picked up his caulking gun and disappeared inside the shower stall. Slammed the door closed.

I flung it open.

Boris?

He swivelled around, the gun trained on my belly. We're talking about standards, Emma. You aren't holding up your end. I have worked like a dog to kick this loft into shape and I'm not sure you even want to live here. You prefer some raw-edged oriental fantasy that has nothing to do with who you are or what I'm comfortable with. Maybe you should –

Your gun's dripping, Boris.

No, what I actually said was somewhat worse. I picked the fight. Boris was squatting, an easy target of ridicule, in the shower-stall, caulking, caulking. I knew I'd been a useless nerd during much of the love-nest reno. I was resisting something, fighting down an image of myself as I actually was, a typical North-American woman about to take the predictable first steps towards a commitment that led to: The. Whole. Package. I never realized how much I loved my irregular nature. My eccentricities, such as they were. The only things separating me from all the women I'd gone to school with. Boris threatened to wipe me out.

My attraction to him was self-mutiny, in a way.

You can't do this to me, I said. I can't let you sacrifice me on the table of love. This loft is a decoy. You intend to live another kind of life. The middle-class blueprint. No more surprises for the next fifty years. I marry you. You get promoted. I get pregnant. I learn how to make soufflés in that oven over there. We turn in early, night after night. My parents ADORE you. The kids are the spittin' image. The bike's traded in on a hatchback. (The word hatchback fuelled me onward.) My wisdom shrivels, is replaced with homilies, recipes, baby talk, little prickles of pride in your achievements while I —

Boris swivelled around to face me, his eyes radiating pained astonishment. How could I tell him that I hadn't rehearsed a word of this outburst, that the sight of his stooped back had triggered my new-found vision of us as — I went on. You are not artistic, Boris. You are not creative. My parents love you more than me. (I stopped. Where had that one come from?) You are just a dry-leaves mind, a presumptuous machine-head, a —

A what, Emma?

— technocrat with a heart like an iron, steaming out

my wrinkles, one by one. You want smooth bed-sheets, not a comPANion!

Emma. You fill me with despair. And horrible doubt. I've been watching you. My work is suffering. You take everything. Nothing comes back. You're a waste of skin. Go home. Grow up. Get out of here.

Boris never sweats. Boris never shouts. Boris never swallows, I sang through the clenched jaws of the elevator and out into the street.

Boris didn't call me at work the next day. I didn't call him.

Two days later a telegram arrived.

The vessel of our love has cracked – Boris.

I relented.

You've done a lot of work, Boris, I said, walking around the loft. I peered into the shower-stall, climbed up the ladder and inspected the new bed. A nest of magazines around his pillow. A heap of reading too, I said, climbing down.

He pulled two sofa cushions onto the floor, took my hand and pulled me down beside me. He held my face in his hands and kissed me, tears in his eyes. I missed you, Emma, he whispered. I'm trying to understand. But you know what I think?

I waited.

I think you should go to Japan.

There it was. Staring up at me. The New York Times. Entertainment section. The black box on the bottom of the second page announcing that Akira was taking his orchestra on tour to Japan. Sometime in early spring. The itinerary listed the major cities but gave no exact dates. April. I'd have to work to get my money by then …

Oh, you'll do that, don't worry, Marjorie said. Call the orchestra. Find out the itinerary. Hell. Call Akira himself. It's been three years. He's probably dying to hear how you're doing. You wait much longer, the guy's likely to have forgotten you completely.

I decided to make the call with cash at a quiet hotel lobby. It was easier than having to explain long distance to Berlin on my parents' bill. Marjorie waited for me in the bar. Information gave me the symphony office number. All I had to do now was pick up the phone, ask for Akira's secretary and explain that I was an old friend. Which I was, wasn't I? I picked up the receiver. Put it down. What would I say? What if they didn't give out that kind of information? What if they put me through to Akira? This was ridiculous. I felt fourteen again. This should be as easy as – this couldn't be harder than going backstage ever was. Plus how else was I going to find out. What if I went all the way over to Japan and couldn't find him?

I dialed the number.

There was a crackle. The operator's voice.

Please deposit three–eighty.

I fumbled with my stack of coins and dropped them. You idiot.

There was a *scriitch* and then a voice in German said something to my operator.

Go ahead please.

My throat was dry. A-Akira Tsutsuma's secretary please.

Long pause.

I'm sorry. Could you repeat that?

I spoke up, glancing around the lobby. Akira Tsutsuma please – I mean his secretary please.

May I help you? It was a woman's voice. Smooth. American-sounding. Yes, I'm an old friend of the Maestro's. A-a neighbour from Toronto. I heard about his Japan tour and I happen to be going over there around that time – I paused and wiped my hand on my shirt, ready for more coins – so if you could give me a sense of his itinerary I'd be able to, to …

Are you connected with the symphony in Toronto?

Ah no, it's strictly a personal ah –

Are you connected with the press in any way?

No, as I said, it's a personal connection only.

I'm sorry, I'll have to check with Mr Tsutsuma first. I can't give out information without permission.

I understand. Can I call back? It'll be kind of hard for you to reach me.

If you wish.

I hung up.

Two days later. Same time, same place.

Hello, it's me again. I called earlier about Mr Tsutsuma's itinerary. Did you get a chance to –

Just a moment. She was riffling through paper. Did that mean?

She was back. Yes, I spoke with the Maestro. He has given me permission. I'll put something in the mail to you. Your address please?

He remembered me! He remembered me! My voice wobbly as I dictated my address. Thanks very much. Wonderful.

She hung up.

I dragged Marjorie off her bar stool in a bear hug.

It worked. I did it.

★

I got to the mail before my folks could and picked up the envelope. A fat one with the orchestra's logo in black and gold at the top left-hand corner which I recognized immediately – and remembered with a guilty start, why. The day after Akira moved out, I had gone back to his house. Bags of garbage were piled up in the back yard. I went through them, rummaging for souvenirs. I couldn't stop myself. I turned up a mass of crumpled correspondence, envelopes with the black and gold logo, love letters in Japanese, signed in English by someone called Makiko, a worn-out pair of conducting slippers, empty cigarette packages, *sake* bottles, magazines, an old turtleneck.

I took the envelope up to my room and tore it open. The itinerary fell out, along with the most neutral of cover letters, signed by his secretary. Enclosed, please find Mr Tsutsuma's itinerary, as requested. Best regards, Ms. J. Appleberg. No message from Akira. No little P. S. Oh well.

Eight pages. He opened the tour in Tokyo, at the — Concert Hall, on April 3rd. Two nights in Tokyo. April 5th. On to Hokkaido. I scanned the place names. None I recognized. Then Bejing, China! A week there. Then back to Honshu. Okinawa. Big hops. He was on the road or in the air virtually every day until the beginning of May, when he returned to Tokyo for two days before flying back to Berlin.

I folded up the letter. What a life. Not much play-time inside that tour. I could try to meet him at the beginning, in Tokyo, but right after that he flew off to Hokkaido. If I missed him in Tokyo, which was entirely possible given the hoopla that usually opened big tours like this one, I knew I couldn't afford to go chasing after him by air. No, Tokyo at the end was my best bet. If I began my trip to coincide with the end of his, I missed the cherry blossoms and risked running into the rainy season. I had just enough money to last me five weeks if I lived on rice and noodles.

I decided to go over at the beginning of April.

Start off in Tokyo, resist the impulse to look him up then. Go on to Kyoto, Nara. See the blossoms. Undertake my pilgrimage properly. Then return to Tokyo. Meet him in that first week of May. And come home.

Already I visualised the backstage entrance of the concert hall, began to rehearse how I would slip through Security, describing myself in terms Akira would recognize when word was carried to him. He was a lot more famous now, but I was older. Authority didn't rattle me quite as much as it had when I'd been a kid. I hoped.

I picked up the phone and began dialling Marjorie. Such decision-making demanded a celebration.

I am in Tokyo. It's the night of our reunion. I am going backstage to meet Akira at last. I head down a long corridor that twists and turns like the contours of an amphitheatre. At last I find the dressing room door with his name in Japanese characters. I knock and then comes that magical moment. He opens the door and his face lights up with joy. *We rush into one another's arms.* We talk for a while and everything seems to be going well but the way he looks at my face is odd. He keeps glancing over at me and then away as if embarrassed slightly. People come by to pick him up so I say goodbye and leave. On the way out I touch my face. Something's wrong. I dash to the bathroom and discover my face is covered in characters painted in mud. I can't read them! There are weeds in my hair too, as though I've been dredged up from the bottom of a pond. How could this have happened to me today, of all days? I am in a panic to know what the characters mean. And furious that my friends could have let me go backstage looking like this. But I have this terrible feeling that I've done it to myself and forgotten.

The Bridge *(Ō-hashi)* of Dreams.

The preparations for flight, extricating myself from my life were a test of my desire. Organizing the money, tickets, clothes and saying goodbye took almost as long as the trip itself would.

I finished my forty-hour evening course in conversational Japanese, quit my job, bought yen, lost my passport, found it, lost it, found it, packed my bags, updated my address book, took a last look around my room, wondering what I'd forgotten. After fantasizing about this trip, eating and breathing it for so long, I was finally only hours away from it at last. My father was rewiring the electricity throughout the house so it was difficult to see during those days. In pure nervousness and haste, I fell down the pitch-dark stairs, carrying my bag to the front door.

Marjorie's cup clinking against mine in the airport lounge. Her toast – 'to the heart.' I remembered all the times I'd heard planes flying overhead and longed to be on one headed for Japan. And now I am strapped into my seat on April Fools' Day, flying to Vancouver. Tomorrow, Japan!

Stewardesses in sarongs, hummingbird bright, pin orchids to our lapels with delicate fingers before turning to push heavy food carts up the aisles like stevedores. Their sarongs are invisibly pleated for ease in bending over us. Everyone drinks non-stop until the artificial night falls and then the stewardesses pull down the blinds and pass out thin blankets.

The plane is descending. Below us, palm trees, flat roofs, bevelled streams, tailored countryside. A dark, unfamiliar green. Even the sky has a green tint to it.

I have landed on Akira's planet.

Narita airport. An hour later I am through.

*

Absolutely stunned with fatigue. My balloon head is attached to my body by a little string. The shops and restaurants are so narrow and only one storey high. I pick up my bag and walk down into the subway. The signs are in both English and Japanese. When the train comes in I am shocked by how small it is inside, rather like a British train, with velour sofas. It is rush hour and I'm packed in with businessmen, wearing identical, old-fashioned pinstriped suits with cuffs, who steal glances at me. No one sits beside me. My shoes are scuffed. I count the stops, three, four, five. This is mine. *Roppongi.* I make up my mind I won't ask for help until I am desperate. Akira. Where are you?

I go outside and hail a taxi. I show the driver my map and the address of the hotel but he seems confused. I was warned that in Tokyo addresses only give a general indication. The street numbers do not relate to one another but rather to when the building was constructed. Streets are under constant reconstruction so maps continually go out of date. The cabbie studies the map for another minute and then gets out and disappears. Leaving me sitting in the cab with the motor running. Fifteen minutes go by. I begin wondering whether or not he's been too shy to ask me to get out and has run off to hide from me, gaijin woman, but I am too tired to get out again. Suddenly there he is, back again. We set off. A few minutes later, he pulls up in front of my hotel. The taxi door and the trunk both swing open automatically and the concierge appears at the curb with a clipboard. I carry my bag after him. Arriving. Always arriving and never quite getting there. I am so tired. But I'm in downtown Tokyo at last.

I'm in bed, floating out my window into the Tokyo night sky.

★

I memorized each corner as I turned it and strolled up and down a dozen blocks as strange as Mars. The streets, the stores, the curbs were out of a dream I'd had a hundred times but never with accuracy. No westerners, no blacks here. An old woman, clutching her shopping bags, passed me in traditional *geta* and kimono. I was too shy to go into a restaurant yet but I passed a stationery store and then backtracked and looked through the window again. I wanted to write letters and keep notes. I went in. Much bowing and greeting by the elderly man behind the counter. I picked up a pen and a notebook and held them up. Ahhh, he said. Pen! Pen! I echoed and waved the note-book. *Ikura desu-ka?* How much? Ahhh, he bowed and wrote the price down on a tiny slip of paper and held it out to me. 250 Y. I had used money for the first time.

I traced my way back to the hotel, noticing that some of the morning's landmarks had disappeared and new ones had taken their place. The rain had got heavy and my head felt thick. I took a hot shower and fell asleep by nine but hunger woke me up again and I went downstairs to the hotel coffee-shop to eat dinner. The western knives and forks on my table were the largest I have ever handled. Like salad tools. They must think gaijin are huge-mouthed giants. I went back to my room and finally fell asleep at five a.m. According to my guide book, nose-blowing is unspeakably offen-sive in this country. What am I to do with this head cold?

I dropped a 100 Y coin into the slot on the tv in my hotel room. The commercials hooked me. I flicked the dial until I found more of them. They ran in a bunch for twenty minutes or so and then didn't come on again for another hour. Technically they looked to be state-of-the-art and much funnier than our own. Famous North Americans were endorsing Japanese products. I saw Andy Warhol, John Travolta and Pat Boone doing spots for videotape, soft drinks, pudding cups. Some of the ads were confusing. Even after several viewings I couldn't spot the product. The best ones combined real with animated: cats on trampolines, penguins weeping from train windows shouting 'Suntory Can Beer-u!,' soya-bean weightlifters heaving an entire baseball team over backwards. A girl in a fluorescent kimono and hi-rise American sneakers, holding her chin in her hands, repeating a nonsense syllable, 'Unh-hunh-hunh-hunh!'

On the street I've been passing teenagers wearing t-shirts chastely printed with English phrases like: 'Just good. Just now. Freckle.' Or, 'Always being high spirits. Anytime keep lively.' Or, 'Impudent Company.' 'Assort, persist, contact.'

In my room I found a magazine with a photograph of a woman in a kimono and voluminous obi. It is nightfall and she is stooping to enter her car. There is rain on the windshield. Her face is in shadow except for a disc of light that illuminates one cheek, leaving legible only an expression of attentive patience with her own awkwardness, caught between two cultures. The photograph draws me back to the day I first imagined myself coming to this place.

A few days later, on the train to Kyoto, I study her face again. She has not changed her expression with time. Even slightly.

I have been trying to leave behind one-yen pieces.
They are almost worthless and take up pocket room. I
left a stack of them on the ledge of a public washroom
only to have an elderly woman come hobbling after
me to return it. I let one drop while standing to catch a
bus and two people instantly stooped to retrieve it for
me. Little, sticky things. I gave up and threw them
into the temple boxes.

A slight hesitancy in speech. I've taken it on to some degree. As though the words get turned around once before finding their way out.

The more I think about myself the more distressed I become. All the more useless since I am so far away from home and I can only make things worse. Rolling matters around in my head just makes them misshapen.

Standing by the driver's mirror, I see my shirt move. That's my breathing! I discover with a pang of joy. I see my shirt move with my breathing. That's me inside that shirt!

I wasn't expecting this.

Almost full moon. I've been mute for days now.

The claustrophobia. A feeling of suffocation inside my own body. I roll around trying to pass this test, of my ability to remain calm, to sleep and breathe at the same time. Below my window, a man sings aloud in the street, his voice bouncing off the tiled roofs. He stops but a cat has found his way to my window and he too begins to howl. My room is a cage, too small to stand up inside, my legs stick out the window. Such cold air, I can see my breath.

I have ordered a bean mush with glutinous rice cake by mistake. My throat balks at the hot sweetness. The salted tangle-seaweed cuts it somewhat, clears my tongue. I pick up my hashi, plunge back in again. Salt and sweetness side by side like spring and fall in my mouth.

What is it I need to know? Remembering the translation of the tea scroll in Daitokuji temple: The flower is red, the willow is green. That is all there is to know.

The motif appears on the tea vessels. The red maple and the cherry blossom. Something dying away and something springing up. Spring and fall occur simultaneously in Japan.

Two days' silence.

After dinner, I strolled through the Gion district to a junction of two historical streets preserved as national treasures. I stood on a bridge and all down the canal, as far as I could see, branches sagging with blossoms trolled in the current. A raft of petals, caught under the bridge, quaked below me. As night fell, the geisha began emerging, making their way to the nightclubs, their *geta* clip-clopping across the cobblestone bridges. Another living woodcut. I walked back to the main street where I passed two well-dressed young men lying face down in vomit. Their girlfriends were huddled together crying. As I walked up the steps to Maruyama Park to see the Weeping Cherry Tree, I passed more drunk couples. It was Saturday night, the last weekend of *Hanami* festival. People had been drinking in the park since sunset or so ... They were dancing in little groups, singing songs, falling down. They have brought tatami matting and portable gas hibachis and jeroboams of *sake* and beer. I passed entire families dozing on their tatami in their party clothes, stretched out like corpses, white socks glowing in the dark.

★

An apparition under floodlights at the top of the hill,

she's surrounded by a bamboo fence – this grand-mother of cherry trees, as tall as a willow. Among the pink blossoms, spikes of delicate green are just begin-ning to poke through. The trunk has been artificially twisted like taffy by gardeners to grow up in a tight spiral. *A spiralled upbringing. Do I share that with her?* The turns do give the tree more height somehow, more of a sense of having grown year by year. Couples emerge from the shadows to take pictures of the tree, then stagger off. Everyone is drunk tonight.

I walk back down the hill past the kiosks selling Fujifilm, *sake,* grilled octopus, decorative live carp and tea. There is a gentleness in the way people are enjoy-ing one another's company – not locked in intellectual conversation but engaged in something else quite sub-tle and different. They are enjoying the air, the blos-soms, the food, their own civility. Petals clog the fountains, flutter over the revellers. I catch one in my *sake* cup.

On the temple steps going out, a couple stands with a remote-control microphone and a cassette deck. Passersby sing into the mike, accompanied by the cassette music. One man holds the book of lyrics up so his wife can read as she sings.

Over the heads of the people on the escalator, I see a poster coming towards me. Akira, hair flying, and the Tokyo orchestra. Flit. Gone.

I should try to call my parents today. I am reading Yukio Mishima's book, full of masculine treachery and manipulative women. The writing has infected my mind with ugly voices and distasteful imaginings. Wanting positive action, I went out and bought my Bullet ticket to Tokyo. I booked a seat on the north side of the train, hoping to see Fujiyama this trip. After lunch I crawled up to the seventh floor of Kyoto Tower hotel to read the *Mainichi, The Japan Times, The Asahi Shinbun* in the coffee lounge. Shirley MacLaine and Robert Duvall have won the Academy Awards. Two days ago was Good Friday. Liberace is visiting China. Canada never makes the news.

Things have changed inside me. The loneliness is gone. I want to hold onto my clear mind. My head is filled with ideas rustling like a dry garden.

In the Higashigawa Lounge there's a glass case with a mannikin dressed in traditional bride's kimonos and headdress. Three old men sit beside it drinking tea, tracing with delicate fingers their bus tour on a map of the city. Every few moments one of them glances over at me, nods politely.

Tonight I feel something welling up that blurs my focus. I have a 100 Y coin for the tv tonight. Power to conjure up company into my room. I mistrust my own imagination – it's gotten in the way, misguided me, made me prey to all kinds of negative thoughts, deluded me into believing – once a cowhand, always a cowhand. Imagination pulling the fabric this way and that to make it fit – like a pushy department store sales- man. I watch the drops of water crawl like larvae down the side of the basin. I've got to stop reading Mishima. I can taste what I've been reading like a malevolent perfume mixed into my food.

The luxurious anticipation of returning … Will I have been missed? How will I tell the stories? Who will want to know everything?. My tattered maps, the kimono, will look incongruous and awkward, laid out on the living-room floor like thoughts pulled out of a dream. *My father, on his knees, howling.*

Japan has been a kind of convalescence.

Golden Week is approaching. Children will be let out of school to go travelling with their families between Kyoto and Tokyo. All the hotels here have been booked months in advance. I will be on my way to Tokyo when it hits, moving upstream.

Tiger mother crossing the ocean with her cubs. The most beautiful of stone gardens, on this gentlest of warm days yet. Thousands of black flies swarm just above the stones as though they were flowers.

The sakura blossoms are sleeting but still at the height of their splendour. I walked through a grove just as the wind blew a pink blizzard sideways into the glossy needles of the pines.

Petals on dark moss. No people here. I walk around Mandarin pond, man-made a thousand years ago. All the mountains reflected in the water belong to the same prefecture of Ryoanji. As I approach a tea-house I hear a bamboo water gong – a sound I'd only read about in haiku. A *pokk* every minute or so as the tube of bamboo, gradually filling with water sluiced from the stream, tips and falls back against a rock. As I walk away, the sound diminishes to a bird chirp.

A young couple are setting up a tripod and camera by a tree. The man rushes to his girlfriend, arm around her shoulder, and just makes it when the click is heard. Instantly, his hand drops. He packs up and they move on to another view.

I am invisible to them. Emma the ghost, hovering just out of frame.

Akira once told me that the south of Kyoto produced the finest tea in Japan so I made inquiries and boarded the train the next morning for Uji. A school group of little children, about forty of them, boarded right behind me and my heart sank. Their teacher made his way to a vacant seat at the far end of the car and sat down with a newspaper and the children flowed towards me like flies to honey and assembled in a tight row of yellow caps, with their name tags and identical black satchels. Each time I made a move they broke into giggles. Their faces came closer and closer until our noses almost touched. Unable to stand their scrutiny a second longer, I pulled out a paperback but each time I turned the page, the group swayed in to see, hoping for pictures perhaps. I prayed that each station we stopped at was theirs but no such luck and it wasn't until we stopped at Uji that they all turned as one and made for the door.

I got out and scuttled across the Uji bridge to put distance between me and my group. Midway across, I had to stop. The view downriver, the mists, the mountains and the rapids, looked like a brush painting, the most exquisite fantasy of Japan. I stood and watched the egrets wheel above the foam.

On the other side, I found an open-air gazebo restaurant overlooking the banks of the river where the wind blew the bamboo curtains in and out as I ate my *zo-sui,* rice gruel, heated over a flame at the table, the young woman who served me brought out *cha-soba,* pickles and *fuki* salad and in hesitant English began to talk. She had heard that Canadians ate something called a pancake with maple syrup and she asked me to describe it. She asked whether I hung my wash outside to dry and why I didn't have children. I made a joke about eating mosquitoes to survive in the bush and her eyes widened with shock. *Western enzymes.* She directed me to a teahouse down the road to have *sencha* and I could barely contain my excitement as I walked towards it – a traditional tea-house – jumping out of the novels I'd read, the woodcuts, the walls I'd dreamed of.

The tea-garden. Freshly sprinkled with water.

Moss, pines, tea-bushes in perfect globes. I pushed the gate aside, stepped onto the slate stepping stones – usually six for practicality, but here, four for *kei* or appearance – leading to the washing basin.

The entrance to the tea-house was small. I had to enter on my hands and knees, then slide on my knees to the right of the entrance. I thought, for god's sake, be careful. You could put your feet through this wall. The room was the size of a doll's house. Tokonoma scroll above the *chabana,* flower arrangement. The hostess entered, bowing. She smiled and pointed to the scroll, translating it roughly as something about bending a flower, the scent entering your clothes, a spring activity. Her movements, as she laid out the tea-things, poured water into the tea-pot, replaced the dipper, poured out the tea into cups, were a celebration of economy, no baroque gestures, no ornamentation. She returned her hands after each small movement to her thighs as though to indicate where the tasks broke into their parts. The tea-cake was made of bean paste mixed with green tea into an emerald fudge. I bowed and watched to see how she ate it with the splinter of wood provided. My cup was filled three times and then it was over. *Don't spill. Don't drop.* She rose and bowed and I bowed and crawled back out into the sunshine, feeling for my shoes under the balcony.

It was sunset now. I walked back across the Uji bridge into the wind, my knees aching, and realized with a pang, that I'd never be back.

When the train pulled into Shichijo station, it was dark. I stood on the bridge and watched the dark ripples below me. For a full day I hadn't thought once about Akira.

In the washroom of the Higashigawa Lounge I found an oblique crack running down the tiled wall. Earthquake? It hadn't been there last week. Outside the train station, students are handing out flyers protesting something. They have been given a police permit to do this. They are standing beside little cherry trees and rose bushes for sale, brought in from the country. Suddenly I see my mother's bleeding-heart bush.

Its name in Japanese means a kind of fish.

Famished for English words I browsed through the foreigners' bookstore and found Jun'ichiro Tanizaki's, *In Praise of Shadows,* an essay on Japanese aesthetics. I found a bench outside the train station and began to read.

Western paper turns away the light, while our paper seems to take it in, to envelop it gently, like the soft surface of a first snowfall. It gives off no sound when it is crumpled or folded, it is quiet and pliant to the touch as the leaf of a tree.

One by one, three transient men came up and fell asleep on the benches around me, the last one escorted there by a policeman who carried his shopping bag of possessions for him.

… The light from the pale white paper, powerless to dispell the heavy darkness of the alcove, is instead repelled by the darkness, creating a world of confusion where dark and light are –

An old woman came up, glanced at the snoring transient and touched my arm. She insisted I share her loaf of white bread, handed me slice after slice in spite of my protests of *'kekko desu.'* I'm full. Then a middle-aged guy, obviously her sidekick, joined us. They exchanged a glance of 'Look what we've got here.' The man peered into my eyes to study their colour. He hadn't seen green ones before. I ate my *pan* and submitted to their scrutiny while I figured out my exit. *'Yakuza'* I pointed, to distract them as I rose, indicating the man with the crutches. They nodded, subdued. Outcasts. All of us.

The ritual was spoiled by my greed today. To be hungry or thirsty at the Tea Ceremony, *Cha-no-yu,* to consume too greedily, was to waste what was offered. I asked for three bowls of tea because the first tasted so good, and poisoned the substance of the ritual. Hunger and thirst also had to be ritualized in order to be satisfied by the ceremony itself. *Cha-no-yu* fed my desire for a ceremony to take place inside me.

I want to bring home rocks and pine seedlings, saffron pickles and cha-soba, katsuobushi shavings, the *sake* cup, gold-flecked, like drinking from a river bottom, the futon tufting piled in the window like milkweed silk, chopsticks cut from bamboo still green and damp, straw sandals with bright rag woven into the straps, shoji paper with fibres, caught smoke that glistens when it's turned to the light, then goes out. Tanizaki's lacquer bowl so light it's like a stomach itself that's lifted to the lips, full of soup. The moisture that gathers under the lid ... The mosaic brick of egg and tofu cooked separately then put together with a seam of fish roe so tiny, pearl grey, it looks like froth so that this one-bite piece resembles a landscape in cross-section to be held but only for a moment between chopsticks before it begins to tear apart.

The Sea of Japan I have been swimming through – this sea of original people – I could swim out of my old life and into a new one, as old as Asia.

A day begun upside down. Mrs. O, the landlady of the Ladies' Inn, comes to bid me goodbye. She gives me a hand-painted tea-cup, wrapped in silver foil, a farewell present. I don't know how to say that she has made a mistake, that I had reserved my room until tomorrow. Caught in my usual awkward web. How would a competent person have solved this, huh? But I have stayed here almost a month, longer than any other guest and I know that during Golden Week she could fit four or five students into my room so, after breakfast, I changed inns and came back to pick up my bags. I presented Mrs. O. with some special tea and two boxes of rice-cakes and my library of Japanese novels in translation and she fell upon Soseki's *I am a cat*. She shook hands and watched me all the way to the end of the street, waving each time I turned around.

Akira, I could jog all the way to Tokyo for you. Listening for your car rumbling up behind me.

The *minshukan* tonight is very modest, run by an *obaasan* and her husband, a kindly-looking pair with absolutely no English. We had tea in their sleeping room while the tv flickered silently on the tatami.

The next morning I waited for half an hour in my room for breakfast, only to discover they had been expecting me downstairs in the sleeping room which was now a dining-room. They sat watching me drink my cold soup, smiling each time I tried another dish, unable to believe I was actually enjoying a Japanese breakfast. The old man leaned forward and crinkled up his face – *'Cohee? Cohee?'* No thanks, I shook my head, *'O-cha, kudasai.'* What! The gaijin preferred green tea to coffee! They patted me on the shoulders. I was really okay.

In the afternoon, I followed the map to Seiteian – a Zen hermitage run by a monk called Shohokku in his house, which was traditional, old and wonderfully shabby, built around an inner garden. I arrived while a meditation sitting was in progress so I knelt by the outer doors and watched the light fade in the garden. When the group rose to do walking meditation, *Kinhin,* I slipped in and joined them. They sat again for fifty minutes, a very long time for me to keep still.

Shohokku's feet were wide and spread into the tatami as though he had walked barefoot most of his life. I couldn't take my eyes off his toes, so beautifully cut. I felt an unseemly sex pang. He asked me to stay for dinner. Young face, deep voice. One of the meditators pointed out Shohokku's wife to me. A nun, she whispered, on leave from her monastery. I looked more closely. She appeared younger than me, very strong lines to her face, serene. As though she had heard us talking, she nodded gravely to me, then got up and disappeared into the kitchen. Shohokku indicated tea and the other meditators rose to follow him into the kitchen. Counting Shohokku and his wife, we made six. The kitchen was ancient, country-style with skylights and gas lamps.

Afterwards we all helped to clean up while the woman who had pointed Shohokku's wife out to me, began to talk incessantly. She was from San Francisco and had been sitting for thirteen years.

We went back into the *sodo* and sat again for an hour. It was easier this time. It surprised me that the San Francisco woman, after such long practice, had to shift position constantly that hour.

I had wanted to ask some questions but I said goodbye and caught the bus back to my *ryokan,* wishing I'd been able to overcome my shyness. I'd lost my one chance to speak to a Zen monk.

On my last afternoon in Kyoto, I toured Nijo Castle but the scale of the architecture was too large to be comfortable in. I walked past hall after hall where the Shogun once received his feudal lords. Mannikins had been arranged to show the Shogun sitting on a dais behind which were panels concealing his bodyguards. Should a disgruntled warlord so much as move towards him in threat, the display card read, the guards would spring out and cut him down. The Shogun's private apartments were austere and cold. He looked lonely, sitting in his floor chair while six ladies-in-waiting bowed on their knees at the far end of the room.

On my way home I came upon a children's cemetery – little spirit-stones with impish faces, wrapped in red cloth aprons with dustcaps on their heads. Offerings had been left which could only have been children's treasures – parts of toys, buttons, crayons, candies.

Looking through a hedge at sunset. Disarray in the garden. Petals in a heap under the rose-bush. Fresh *fuki* leaves thrown into a compost pit. As the sun burned below the horizon I remembered that there had been a time when I would have wanted to hold onto such a moment, preserve it in memory's amber. Tonight there was only the experience.

In the Noh drama I'd seen that afternoon, four characters served tea to an itinerant monk. This took thirty-five minutes. In the second act, two men each tried to persuade a small child to follow him. Several of the attendants nodded fast asleep as they sat onstage. After a lengthy soliloquy, the percussion and flute began to play and a feeling of 'thus it was' transformed the soliloquy into the sound of a soliloquy. I wondered now if I had understood any of it correctly at all.

I was musing thus, when I turned around to walk home and discovered that all the landmarks I used by day had been swallowed up in darkness. For over an hour I wandered up and down identical streets searching for something I might recognize. Finally I gave up and sat down on the curb. A housewife came up to me. I showed her my address card and she smiled, hand over mouth, and pointed across the road. Silly gaijin, led home by the hand.

An old woman's voice from the window, singing the Tanka love songs from the New Year's game, *Hyaku nin i-shu,* one hundred people, one head.

On the train to Tokyo, I caught my reflection in the mirror as we entered a tunnel, my features distorted into exactly the grotesque gaijin mask I feared I wore. Big hair, tiny face. Long nose, round eyes, jutting chin. Little pinhead, big mouth, goose neck.

I looked away, my thoughts in a jumble ... a mountain of pine needles, children's graveyard, countless yellow caps, Akira, my own harsh voice, my unchanging thoughts, useless fantasies of wanting to change form, my expressions of taste, hungry-spirit torture, restless craving. My judgement of other people, the endless comparing, a process relentlessly refineable.

Tanuki, the badger, changed form into a tea-kettle, allowing his master to sell him to a monastery. A young monk began scrubbing the sooty kettle, whereupon the *tanuki-cha-gama* began protesting – 'Not so hard!' The startled monk rushed off to tell his master, who advised him to put the kettle on to boil. When the heat became unbearable, the *tanuki* changed back to his original badger form and ran away.

The passenger told me that story, he said, in order to explain the Japanese mind. I needed to appreciate the animism of Japan, particularly of rural Japan. He talked about the extremism of his people. Their tendency to be overly rigorous in their cleanliness, work ethic. The Japanese cares about what his good neighbour thinks of him and what his bad neighbour thinks. Ego is very weak, he said. This is a problem of the Japanese.

I remembered the *obaasan* at the *minshuku.* Her practiced hands pulling together Juniper branches, dahlias, an iris, baby's breath, into a tokonoma arrangement. Tall, to complement the scroll. She showed me how to hold the bowl, her fingers cool as they closed over my own.

'*Pon.*' The sound the cha-whisk handle made each time she dropped it against the rim of the tea bowl. When I tried to stand up afterwards, both my legs were completely asleep. I pointed to them and shrugged, made a thumbs down, no dice, gesture. She caught on and laughed out loud, hand over mouth, shoulders shaking. She asked me, like so many other people, what I came here for. *Pon*. A feeling of completing a natural ring of stones. Every thing here, every fold, colour, shape, position, stones and flowers, pottery – gives this pleasure.

I took the newspaper with the announcement of Akira's concert downstairs to the concierge.

Please, would you give me directions?

He studied it for a moment then got out a sheet of paper.

The — Concert Hall is in Oueno district. You know Oueno station?

I nodded.

We are here. You get out here. He tapped his map with a pencil. Take east exit. Walk two blocks. To here. He tapped. You must buy ticket first. You like me to call?

I nodded. How much are the tickets?

You want best seat? Orchestra section?

I nodded.

He scanned the ad some more. Ah. Six thousand yen.

I'd like to reserve one for tonight, please.

He wrote it down.

I call you. You want to pick up ticket at box office, before concert?

He said concert just the way Akira used to. Cone-a-saht.

Please.

No problem.

I went back upstairs to wash my hair, get flustered, get unflustered, organise my costume, do something with my eyes. I wanted to look terrific. Without looking conspicuous. Women didn't wear much makeup here. They didn't travel on the subway dressed to the nines.

Oh, Marjorie, I wish you were here with me.

Seven o'clock.

I went out and ate dinner. I felt calm now. Unnaturally so. I pretended it was just another dinner for one at my Roppongi noodle house. Should I drink *sake* or not?

I decided to have one *tokkuri*. A little carafe. To steady myself. To get loose enough to enjoy this exercise. I sucked the noodles in, cursing the way I was already beginning to revert to my old geeky self. Just as clumsy and self-conscious as ever. After a certain point, it was obvious, growing up wasn't going to have any further effect on me. Years stacked on top of my experience could be peeled back like a sardine lid to reveal – voila! – the same little person peeking out from under. Floundering in the oil of her own foolishness.

I looked at my watch. Seven-forty. Time to get changed.

I got back to my room, peeled the cellophane off my dry-cleaning. A black dress. Stockings. Flat shoes. Hair pinned up. Not unlike the costume I had often worn backstage at home. Not so fancy that I got hopelessly self-conscious, nor so precarious that I was likely to trip or catch my sleeve on a doorknob. Appropriately subdued for this country.

I took one last look in the mirror before locking the

door behind me. Relax, Emma. If you don't get to see him tonight, there's always tomorrow. But I knew it had to be tonight.

Oueno station was its typically nightmarish self with mysterious exits and sub-levels I always mistook for the one I wanted. Even though I thought I'd followed the concierge's directions perfectly I had to stop and ask a passerby on the street. I showed her the newspaper clipping.

Her face lit up. Ah so! Maestro Tsutsuma. Berlin Symphony Orchestra!

She pointed.

Two blocks. Not far. Her smile melted me. Everyone reminded me of A. right now.

I thanked her and began to trot towards the hall.

I found the box office and repeated my name at the window. Slid my yen through. The ticket was printed in Japanese.

I was shown my seat and given a programme. And there was his face on the cover. Wow! He had aged. His hair was mostly grey now. Akira, your life has been rough on you. His face was lined around the eyes and mouth, fatigue lines that looked western.

I scanned the programme. Dvorak's fourth. My god. The last concert I'd ever seen him conduct. I had bought the record afterwards just so I could cry again over the oboe solo, trying to recall everything that night watching him on the podium, trying to memorise his gestures, clinging to him. Such clinging.

People around me were fanning themselves with their programmes. Most people wore western dress. This was a western cultural event, after all, but a few old women wore formal kimono and obi. Nodding to one another, their fans tucked into their obis. It was a setting I had pictured to myself a thousand times and now it was –

The hall darkened. A knife-thin figure darted onstage, pushing back a mop of hair with one hand, stooping slightly as he moved. He stepped up onto the podium, faced the audience and bowed. It was a Japanese bow. Deeper. A perceptible pause before coming up again. The audience applauded, then stopped abruptly. He had picked up his baton.

How can I describe the feelings those opening bars brought back? An instant re-enactment of that moment, so long ago, when he had first walked onstage into my life. Look at him, Emma. Look at him. My eyes filled with tears, reconstituting cells I thought had long since died. And yet...

The concert was over. Akira waved the orchestra to its feet and bowed again, hand over heart. The audience loved him, their home-grown boy. They brought him back again and again and then finally the house lights came on and people began to gather up their things and make their way up the aisles to the doors.

I jumped out into the aisle and swam upstream to the front of the stage where I found the side exit and the hallway leading to the backstage entrance. A guard stood in front of the door.

Excuse me. I'd like to meet Maestro Tsutsuma. I said in Japanese.

He held open the door for me and instantly an usher appeared on the other side. They whispered together and then the usher beckoned to me. This was going to be easier than I thought. I followed him down the labyrinth, past harp cases and percussion stands, players lounging about, their ties unravelled, smoking cigarettes, stagehands stacking chairs, gathering up scores. The usher pointed me towards a throng of people, all dressed very formally, holding large flower arrangements, standing outside the Maestro's door. They looked like young musicians with their teachers or parents, everyone very nervous and excited, much shifting of the bouquets, clearing of throats. I realized again how much more famous Akira had become in the last few years, and especially over here. These people were preparing to meet a royal personage and their nervousness made me smile and almost relax. Maybe I was the only one who actually knew Akira – the guy. Whose car stalled on the hill in the winter. Who locked his dry-cleaning in the trunk and lost the key. Who laughed on the telephone and lost his balance, pushed the button down with his knee and disconnected himself. Who was on the other side of this very door.

The crowd inched forward. I heard him long before I caught sight of him, greeting people as they came in, speaking rapid Japanese, his voice gravelly with fatigue. His end-of-tour voice. One by one, his fans re-emerged without their flowers, their faces glowing. I leaned against the wall, patient to be last. Finally, the usher signalled to me. My turn.

I stood in the doorway, programme in hand. He was sitting, my solitary Shogun, surrounded by flowers, pen in hand. Blue kimono, hair glossy with sweat. I handed him my programme and he took it, glanced up for an instant and then back down. Then he looked up again. His face fell. A classic double take.

Emma!

Hello, Akira. I said.

We talked for almost an hour. I asked him about his tour, his orchestra, life in Europe. He was a family man now. It had been in the papers back home. He asked about the street, had anything changed. Was I married and how were my parents. Catch-up talk that veered away from being very personal. Unconsciously, I found I'd reverted to the way I used to talk to him, in shortened, simple phrases, dropping the articles, as he did.

From time to time, his Japanese manager peeked in, said something and disappeared again, leaving us to ourselves a little while longer. Finally he said, I must change.

I stood up. He'd given me so much time already.

You must be tired. I'll leave you now.

He took my hand and held it. Looked for a long time into my face.

Are you happy? Your life, is it good?

A shadow flitted across his face. It's hard work being conductor. Always lots of meetings with management, lots of responsibility. Not enough sleep. I am tired often. He laughed. I am old man, Emma. Old, old man now. Please! You laugh at me!

I couldn't help it. I squeezed his hand.

I should let you go.

But Manager and some symphony people are going to dinner now. You must come. If you have time. I am so happy to see you, Emma.

I nodded. I'd love to.

But our intimacy was over. I knew exactly what the next two hours would be like. Akira as the gracious host-maestro. The cavalcade of cars to the restaurant, the seating arranged diplomatically, most important people next to him. The food and drinks pre-ordered for our group. The mixed up introductions in English and Japanese, most of the dinner spent making conversation with strangers on either side of me, musicians, the princes and princesses of culture inquiring eventually, what instrument did I play, or was I somehow, family, and he, the perfect host, always monitoring, leaning across to rescue me, putting me in context for them – She was old neighbour, small girl once, this big, – his hand indicating, his graceful, golden hand with flat nails – and now she is lovely young woman. Careful not to create any incorrect notion of our relationship.

Yes, I could have added, once I was secretly in love with Akira. I used to keep a log of his comings and goings, the clothes he wore. I saved his hair. I once stood at the top of the street with a stack of records in my hand, waiting to ambush him coming home from rehearsal. When he moved away I thought my heart would break and I flipped out.

And why had I come here? To tell him everything he had meant to me, how he had haunted my life? And for him to tell me why a man like him had befriended me in the first place, who I'd been to him? In order for me to separate the past from the present. I didn't know. To kill Akira? Kill the Buddha! Shohokku, the Zen monk had shouted in the meditation hall. The moment He becomes an impediment to your practice, a concept instead of a real person.

But here, seeing him again, I understood, finally, that that conversation was never meant to be. I didn't need to know. And then it came over me – but by degrees, seeping into my hold, compartment by compartment.

It was over.

This dinner would end and I would go back to my hotel, put my costume away, get into bed. Tomorrow

I would spend any way I liked, to follow my big feet down into the Shinjuku district and use up my last yen buying presents for my family and fly home. It was time to debrief. To move the needle to a new scratch.

Suddenly I couldn't wait to go. To say goodbye, and hail a cab out of here. I stood up.

It's late, I have to go now.

He held out his hand.

I came around the table and held it, conscious of the eyes on us. I squeezed it and let it go.

Bye-bye.

Bye-bye Emma. Thank you. You go back soon to Canada?

Thursday afternoon.

So soon. His eyebrows lifted. You must give your parents my best regards.

I nodded. Of course.

Auf Wiedersehen, Emma.

I laughed. Auf Wiedersehen, Akira.

Until I see you again.

Born in 1953, Sarah Sheard is a recent winner of the "Forty-five Below" competition, which placed her among Canada's top ten young fiction writers. Her stories have appeared in numerous magazines and anthologies throughout Canada. *Almost Japanese* is her first novel. For three years Sarah Sheard has taught creative writing in "The Dream Class," a special program for talented Canadian high school students, originated eight years ago by her husband, novelist David Young. A member of a Zen Buddhist temple in Toronto, the mother of an infant son, and an avid swimmer, Ms. Sheard writes short fiction erotica in her spare time and is completing a new novel composed of family and neighborhood portraits.